Books by Betty Hager

The Gift of the Dove
Old Jake and the Pirate's Treasure
Miss Tilly and the Haunted Mansion
Marcie and the Shrimp Boat Adventure
Marcie and the Monster of the Bayou

Musicals by Betty Hager

Angels, Lambs, Ladybugs, and Fireflies
    (with Fred Bock)
A Super Gift from Heaven (with Fred Bock)
Three Wee Kings (with Dan Sharp and
    Fred Bock)
The Greatest Christmas Card in the Whole,
    Wide World (with Fred Bock)
O, My Stars, It's Christmas! (with Fred
    Bock and Anne Claire)
God with a Capital G (with Fred Bock)
The Mall and the Night Visitor (with Fred
    Bock)
God's Rainbow Promises of Christmas (with
    Fred Bock)
Hallelujah 1-4-8 (with Fred Bock)
Angels, Lambs, Caterpillars, and Butterflies
    (with Fred Bock)
Holiday Inn, Bethlehem (with Fred Bock)

MISS TILLY and the HAUNTED MANSION

BETTY HAGER

ZondervanPublishingHouse

Grand Rapids, Michigan

A Division of HarperCollinsPublishers

Miss Tilly and the Haunted Mansion
Copyright © 1994 by Betty Hager

Requests for information should be addressed to:
Zondervan Publishing House
Grand Rapids, Michigan 49530

Library of Congress Cataloging-in-Publication Data

Hager, Betty.
    Miss Tilly and the haunted mansion / Betty Hager.
        p. cm. — (Tales from the bayou)
    Summary: Four children in Alabama discover that Miss Tilly,
reputed to be a witch, is really just a lonely old woman.
    ISBN 0-310-38411-7 (pbk.)
    [1. Witches—Fiction. 2. Old age—Fiction. 3. Cajuns—Fiction.
4. Alabama—Fiction.] I. Title. II. Series: Hager, Betty. Tales
from the bayou.
PZ7.H12416Mi   1994
[Fic]—dc20   93-45726
                                                             CIP
                                                             AC

Edited by Lori J. Walburg
Cover designed by Cindy Davis
Cover illustration by Doug Knutson
Interior illustrations by Craig Wilson, the Comark Group

Printed in the United States of America

94 95 96 97 98 / DH / 10 9 8 7 6 5 4 3 2 1

For Mark, Jenny, Jessica,
Stephen, and Matthew,
because I love them

Contents

A Witch?

Y ou don't have to believe me if you don't want to," Pierre Delacruz said to my brother, Raymie, "but I oughta know. I live next door to her. Miss Tilly's a witch, for sure. You wouldn't believe the things that happen at her house."

Pierre was small for his age. He was twelve, two whole years older than I was, but he wasn't any taller than I. He was small and dark, with a mass of black, curling hair framing his thin, sharp face. My friend, Jeanné, thought he was nice. We had sympathetic feelings for him, because he didn't have a mother, and he had a sort of helpless look about him.

The day we heard him talking about Miss Tilly was the last day of school, May 30, 1933. Jeanné and I were following along behind my brother,

9

Raymie, and his friend, Hank, as they talked to Pierre. We tried not to walk too closely behind them. They were both fifteen, and we didn't want them to tell us to get lost.

"Aw, come off it, Pierre," Hank said. "You telling those ole ghost stories about Miss Tilly's house again? You're full of crazy beans."

"It's the truth. Honest," Pierre said. He made an X on his chest. His eyes were big and his expression was solemn. "Have you seen that ole woman lately? Scare you to death. Body all crumpled up. No teeth. Eyes with spooky, dark circles under them. She's a witch, I tell you."

Even on that sun-filled day, something about that word *witch* sent chills zinging down my back. I couldn't help butting in, even though I knew Raymie and Hank would give me dirty looks for eavesdropping.

"Maybe you shouldn't call her a witch, Pierre," I said. "That's not a nice thing to say about anyone."

But despite my holier-than-thou attitude, I was as curious as the next person.

Pierre lowered his voice and looked around to see if anyone else was walking nearby. Then he said in a raspy voice, "I am not telling you folks a fib. There are sounds coming out of that house that would send chills from your pointed ears to your stubby toes. Why, I've seen . . ."

He paused and looked at Jeanné and me. I

think he was proud to be walking home from school with these fifteen-year-old boys, but he didn't mind including us; he liked an audience.

His eyes grew narrow. He whispered when he finished the sentence . . . "*unbelievable* things . . . things that would scare you so bad your hair would turn white overnight."

I wondered why *his* hair hadn't turned white. "Why?" I asked. "What things?"

"Yeah," Jeanné asked, "like what?"

We all stopped on the sidewalk then. We had come to the small main street of my hometown, Bayou La Batre, Alabama. We'd be separating here. Pierre would go straight over the bridge to Sea Trout Lane where he lived. We'd be going down the white, crushed-oyster-shell road to our home. Hank and Jeanné usually took a short cut through the woods at this point. They both lived on Moss Oak Road.

We gathered in a circle around Pierre. He was determined to defend his honor.

"Listen," he said. "Y'all come to my house tomorrow, and I'll prove it." He gave a short, affirmative nod to his head, putting an exclamation point on his story.

This was a dare. It's not easy to let a dare slip past a ten-year-old, but at Raymie's and Hank's age? Impossible.

Raymie said, "Aw, you're just bumping your gums together to hear them squeak."

11

I felt sorry for Pierre. He had a sensitive, little-boy manner about him that made me want to defend him.

"You're just scared, Raymie," I taunted, tossing my head at him in a saucy way.

Hank gave me a dirty look and said, "Yeah, Marcie, if you're so brave, shrimp, why don't you go? You and your little towhead friend here?"

Jeanné put her hands on her hips and leaned forward, sticking her sharp little chin up. "Well, maybe we will, Hank Thompson," she said. As skinny as she was, she looked as if she would take on Hank and Raymie together.

"Yeah," I breathed, but I'll have to admit, I wasn't sure I wanted to face a witch without my older brother.

Pierre was determined to show us he wasn't making up lies. "I'll tell you what," he said, "If I'm not telling the truth, I'll give each of you a quarter for the picture show."

This was too good an offer to miss. Mickey Rooney was playing at the movie house that week. He was awful popular right then because times were hard and he helped people to laugh.

"All right," Raymie said. "You've got a deal."

We shook on it, and Raymie and I walked home talking about it all the way.

At dinner we told Mama and Papa about Pierre and Miss Tilly. Mama shook her head. "I think it's terrible that poor boy has to stay there all alone in the house when Mr. Delacruz and his big brother are out shrimping. Living there alone like that, it's no wonder he tells those wild stories. He has an imagination just like Marcie's."

I should have taken that as a compliment, but I didn't.

Papa looked at us sternly. "Now, don't you be bothering Miss Tilly. Remember the trouble you got in when you trespassed on Mr. Jake's property last year."

We nodded guiltily. We had gone in Mr. Jake's house looking for a treasure map. I felt awful bad when I thought about how rude we were to poor Mr. Jake back then.

Mama shook her head. "I told you when you said Mr. Jake was a ghost that there was no such thing," she said. "But you wouldn't believe me."

"That was just a case of mistaken identity," Raymie said.

That's the answer he gave when the subject of "Old Jake" came up. We politely called Old Jake "Mr. Jake" now. All of us southerners pronounced it "Mistuh," and that became his name.

Mr. Jake used to be homeless, but now he lived in the shed off our washhouse. Mama and Papa had fixed it up really nice for him. There was a toilet and a washbowl in there, and they had bought a comfortable bed for him.

He helped Papa in his Marine Hardware and Supply Shop on the bayou across from our house.

He ran errands for Mama and did a little gardening. He was good at growing vegetables, and he helped Mama with the flowers.

Now that he lived on our property, we had almost forgotten how we had thought he was some kind of evil apparition. Still, Mr. Jake had nothing to do with Miss Tilly. For all we knew, she really *was* a witch!

Saturday morning Jeanné and I started off early for Pierre's house. Hank and Raymie were going to come later. Raymie had to help Papa "oil up" the shrimp boats that were going out to the Gulf of Mexico. Hank worked for Mr. Beaudreaux at the drug store early Saturday mornings.

As frightened as we were, Jeanné and I felt a wonderful excitement.

"Do you think Miss Tilly's a witch?" Jeanné asked.

"Nah," I said, "I don't believe in witches and ghosts."

I wasn't certain what I believed, but Mama was positive she was right about this. I wanted to be right, too.

But I had to admit, I was afraid of Miss Tilly. Pierre had given a good description of her. All of us were afraid of her.

To get to Pierre's house we had to either row across the bayou or go through town and eventually cross Grand Pont. That's French for Big

Bridge. Actually, it wasn't very big, but it looked big to Jeanné and me.

Grand Pont was a drawbridge. When a boat with a tall mast needed to go through, Mr. Henson, the bridge keeper, pushed a button that made the bridge divide into two parts. The parts would lift into the air and make room for the mast.

Jeanné and I hesitated at the bridge for a long time.

"Suppose Mr. Henson doesn't see us and it starts going up, just when we reach the top?" Jeanné asked.

We always worried about that. I knew exactly what she meant. Every time I crossed I would imagine that bridge opening just as I got to the place where it divided.

Today was no different. We stopped and looked at the boats, pretending interest in all sorts of things we usually didn't notice.

"Ooh, look at these pretty flowers," I said. I stopped to examine wild pink primroses growing by the side of the road. Jeanné "oohed" and "ahhed" just as if this were the first time she had ever seen primroses.

But as I looked at the primroses, I didn't really see them. I saw myself on the bridge as it began to open. My thoughts painted a startlingly clear picture of me, grasping the edge of one side, clinging as the gap widened. I could see the black waters of the bayou through the ever-widening gap. I held on with all my strength, but my hands weakened; I lost my grip. My screams pierced through the morning air as my body plunged into the bayou below. The shock and fear were too strong; I drowned.

I didn't realize that, as I took my last, drowning breath, I gurgled out loud.

Jeanné heard. She took one look at me and clutched my arm.

"Something bite you?"

I was embarrassed. I giggled. I assured her I hadn't been bitten by a mosquito, a thousand-legger, or a snake.

But just as we were beginning to cross she caught my hand and whispered, "Oooh, Marcie, maybe it'll open up just as we get to the middle, and it'll go up, and, oh, my goodness, what if we land, *kersplatt*, on a shrimp boat below?"

I whispered my own gruesome thought, "Yeah, maybe right now Miss Tilly is putting a hex on us!"

Jeanné stopped and stared at me with glittering eyes.

"She couldn't know we're crossing right this minute, could she? Why, she doesn't even know we're coming," she said.

I wasn't sure. I didn't say anything.

"Well, does she?" Jeanné pressed for my answer.

16

"If she's a witch, why not?" I finally answered. My eyes narrowed, my voice lowered.

"Maybe she'll cause us to fall on the pointed top of the mast. Then we'll be dead fish, for sure. All broken bones, and smushed flesh and icky blood."

I shivered.

Jeanné shivered.

That vivid picture flashed so strongly in our imaginations that we held tightly to one another's hands and started running, with all the energy we could bring forth, to the other side.

Just as we reached the middle, something happened. We both fell. Was the bridge actually opening? Had our fears come true?

No. Jeanné had tripped and fallen over the small strips of metal at the place where the sides joined; the bridge hadn't moved.

We looked over to the operator's booth where Mr. Henson sat, calmly drinking a cup of coffee. He lifted a lazy hand and waved at us, smiling.

Safely across the bridge we began to speculate again. The frightening possibilities swept over us.

Did she know where we were? Had she cast a spell on us as we crossed? Was she a witch? A ghost? Maybe even a vampire?

"Do you think Pierre's telling us the truth?" I asked.

Jeanné nodded her head vigorously. "He must

be. He doesn't seem the sort who would just make things up to scare people."

We walked down a narrow, dirt road between a row of ancient, gnarled oaks. Even on this morning of blue skies and billowing, white clouds, the trees cast darkened shadows on the road.

At Water Moccasin Bayou we turned onto Sea Trout Lane. When we came to Pierre's house he told us his papa and his brother were out shrimping in the Gulf of Mexico on their boat, the *Lillie Mae*.

Pierre gave us some day-old corn bread to munch on while we waited for Hank and Raymie. Cold corn bread certainly wasn't my favorite treat, but it didn't taste too bad with blackberry jam.

We thought Raymie and Hank would never get there. They were probably "horsin' around," as Cuddin Cassie would say. *Cuddin* was the way we pronounced *cousin*.

"Why don't we just walk past Miss Tilly's house while we're waiting?" I suggested to Jeanné and Pierre.

"That'd be okay," Pierre said, so the three of us ambled past the house, hoping we'd see her and praying we wouldn't.

That old house gave me the creepiest feeling I had ever had. We didn't get on that side of the bayou often, and I didn't remember ever passing the house and seeing it in full view.

I took Jeanné's arm and whispered, "Look at that, Jeanné."

"Yeah," she sighed.

We had never seen such a house. In Mobile there were some fine houses on Government Street, really big. But various add-ons over the years gave this house the appearance of being larger than most.

The house was even more frightening than that narrow, two-storied house Mr. Jake had lived in before it burned. I had thought his house was spooky, but Miss Tilly's was like the haunted houses illustrated in storybooks.

I could see this had been a mansion at one time, and like I said, it rambled on and on. There were two stories, but the cupolas, widow's walks, and turrets made the house unlike any others in our town.

Besides being weird and unusual, the entire place was in a bad state of decay. The wood crumbled in places, and who knew when it had last been painted? The most recent color had probably been white, but most of the paint had peeled and was now a sickly, greyed-green.

We couldn't see the house clearly from the road. There was an overgrowth of weeds and shrubs.

An old magnolia tree near the door was larger than the big one in our front yard. Its limbs were twisted, more like the limbs of an ancient oak.

One of the branches leaned so close to the roof it seemed to rest there.

Because of the frequent rains and the extreme humidity of southern Alabama, some of the houses in Bayou La Batre had tin roofs. Miss Tilly's tin roof was beginning to rust.

I'd never seen a house with as much climbing jessamine growing on it. There were trellises built on all sides and on every curve and corner.

The house was quiet. If Miss Tilly was home, there was no sign of her.

Jeanné wasn't a coward, but she didn't always share my sense of adventure. Mama said Jeanné was more prosaic, whatever that meant.

Jeanné's voice was kind of shaky when she said to Pierre, "Let's go on back to your house. I'm thirsty."

Impatient, I said, "Oh, Jeanné, you can get a drink anytime." I didn't want to miss a single, precious moment of looking at this old place. Frightened, but loving the feeling, I said, "Why don't we just go a little bit closer? Maybe ring the doorbell and see what happens."

"No!" Jeanné recoiled, "You promised your mama."

I didn't argue. In fact, I was kind of relieved. We started walking back, mostly backward, keeping our eyes on that monstrous old house with mounting interest.

Eventually Hank and Raymie showed up,

acting silly and "horsin' around," just as I'd expected.

When we were settled and had given the boys a detailed account of what we'd seen, we started out to investigate Pierre's rumors.

The few acres between Miss Tilly's and Pierre's couldn't be called a *vacant* lot. There wasn't a house built there, but there were so many scrub pines that Miss Tilly's house couldn't be seen from Pierre's. Around every pine was a thick growth of weeds, and shrubs, and a variety of wild plants. Blackberry vines, climbing wild roses, wisteria, and the thick, tangled vines of wild grape grew there.

I tucked this information away into a couple of memory cells in my brain. Jeanné and I would certainly want to come back here to pick blackberries, grapes, and wildflowers another time.

We quietly crept our way through this mass of unruly growth. Close to the house we hid behind a thick bush where we could peer out at the ramshackled mansion.

Nervous, I asked Raymie, "We're not going to trespass, are we?"

"Oh, shut up, Marcie," he said rudely. "We're just looking . . ."

Sometimes I didn't like my brother even a little bit.

At first we couldn't see anything, just the sun shining on the windows. Then we noticed a strange, hazy . . . *something* . . . upstairs. There was definitely a filmy, white mass moving around there. And there were eerie sounds wafting from the room.

Later, when we told Mama about it, she said the wind was probably blowing the curtains, or maybe Miss Tilly was singing, but Jeanné and I didn't believe that. After all, Mama wasn't there to know firsthand the way we were. The song was slow and mournful; it had to be the song of a wailing ghost. What else?

There were goose bumps over every inch of my body.

Raymie suddenly pushed at me and said, "*Rowrr!*"

I almost fainted. "Stop that!" I cried.

Jeanné and I held hands. Tightly. We stopped to listen, and that's when the figure appeared at the upstairs window.

A terrible face stared out at us. A thin, gaunt face, etched with a million wrinkles. And, just like Pierre had said, there were wide, dark circles around the eyes. She really *didn't* have teeth. Her face sunk in at her mouth as deeply as it did at her eyes.

Strange.

Gruesome.

Then, mysteriously . . . she disappeared.

"Come on, let's go," Raymie whispered.

At first we didn't move. But then, giggling

nervously, we turned to run. As we passed Miss Tilly's back door she came out, flailing a broom.

Cackling.

Screeching.

"You kids get on home, you hear me?"

We scattered as swiftly as frightened birds, our feet flying. We stumbled through the bushes, scratching our legs and arms, not daring to look back. Even Hank and Raymie ran. Hank and Raymie, who would never admit to being afraid of anything or anyone.

At Pierre's house we sat on the back steps, our bare feet in the powdery dust of his yard. He gave us each a small bottle of Coca Cola. The coke wasn't cold; Pierre hadn't gone to the ice house that weekend. That was because he had to carry it all the way back across Grand Pont in a wagon; his papa couldn't afford to have ice delivered.

We were so hot and perspiring we didn't care about the coke being warm. We were grateful to have something wet. Our tongues were dry from fear and excitement. For the first time I knew what Papa meant when he said something made him "scared spitless."

After a while, Raymie said, "You know, she's just an ole woman. Real ole. Almost a hundred, Mama says. I don't think she's a witch or anything."

Maybe if I hadn't wanted to believe in the idea of something as scary as a witch, I would have listened to the kindness in Raymie's voice. I was always ashamed later when I'd pay attention to my bad thoughts.

But I said, "Well, you just tell me this, Smarty Pants. Who else would chase folks away with an ole, battered broom? A witch. That's who!"

The Carnival

T wo weeks after school let out for the summer, a carnival came to town.

Mama said I could go with Jeanné if her mama said she could go. Jeanné's mama said that'd be fine if we got home before the sun went down.

Jeanné and I met halfway between our houses. We could scarcely keep ourselves from screaming and shouting with glee as we walked. The carnival was across the street from the picture show. That's what we called the movie house.

Papa gave me a dollar, and Jeanné's papa gave her fifty cents. We had both saved a little from the occasional money we'd earn doing small jobs for our folks. A nickel here. A penny there. Together we had almost three dollars.

At three in the afternoon Jeanné and I stood gaping at the Ferris wheel. There were only three rides: the merry-go-round, the Ferris wheel, and the whip.

The whip was fun and kind of scary, but ever since the time I snapped my neck back and couldn't turn my head for a week, I sort of lost interest in riding that one.

Jeanné and I rode the merry-go-round four times. The rides cost a nickel each.

"Wanna throw the bean bag and win a stuffed animal?" I asked.

I was feeling a little sick from going in circles on that merry-go-round for four times and eating a hot dog with sauerkraut, ketchup, and mustard. Oh, and yes, we'd had a coke and a big, pink puff of cotton candy. For some reason it wasn't mixing too well with the hot dog and coke.

"How about the Ferris wheel next?" Jeanné asked.

The Ferris wheel was our favorite. We thrilled with pleasure when our seat stopped at the top. We'd move back and forth, swaying our seat as we forced ourselves to lean over and look down from the height.

"Nah," I said, moistening my lips, trying to forget my queasy stomach. "Let's throw the bean bag and then ride the Ferris wheel, if it's okay with you."

We went over to a booth where wooden rabbits

went round and round on a raised wheel. The spokes faced us, and I was sure I could hit one of those rabbits. If you hit a yellow rabbit, you'd win the big striped zebra. The blue, pink, lavender, and pale green rabbits were next. I aimed for the pink because I wanted that little white puppy more than I wanted the zebra.

I leaned back, squinted my eyes, and threw. I missed. Every time I threw, I missed. I spent three whole nickels trying to win that puppy.

"Let me try," Jeanné said.

As disappointed as I was, I knew I should save my money for the Ferris wheel and a rainbow ice cream cone, so I moved over to let her try.

She gave the man her money. I could tell by the way she was screwing up her face that she was trying as hard as I had. Later, we decided the carnival man ran the rabbits faster every time it looked as if we were going to hit one.

"That man is a selfish cheater, Jeanné," I said, thrusting my lower lip out in disgust as we walked away.

"He sure is," she agreed.

I remembered then that Mama had told me I'd be foolish to play those target games.

"There's no way you'll win, honey," she said.

"Well, I've seen people win," I argued.

"Well, sometimes they let you win," she said, smiling, "but when you do, those stuffed animals

28

are so cheap they fall apart as soon as you get one."

I sighed. I knew she was right, but I loved the way that little fluffy puppy looked.

We got in line for the Ferris wheel, and as soon as the giant wheel came to a stop we paid our nickel and scrambled into the seat, giggling with excitement.

The first ride was exciting. Jeanné was so daring about swaying our seat that the wheel operator scolded us when our seat stopped for a while at the bottom.

"Y'all keep that up and I'm gonna make you git off," he warned.

We weren't the kind of kids who deliberately disobeyed grown-ups, so we settled down a little, but on the second ride we almost forgot. The "Carny Man," as we called him, grinned at us when we asked to buy a third ticket.

"I know you little ladies like to have fun," he said, "but this time I'm gonna stop the wheel for sure if y'all don't behave."

We promised.

After all the seats were filled the Carny Man came back over to us. Our swing seat was waiting at the bottom. We had been behaving. We looked at him, our eyes big with concern.

"Y'all mind if this here lady goes with you?" he asked. "There ain't no more room, and she's 'bout to have a fit to give her baby a ride."

29

Jeanné and I looked at one another. We didn't want to share our Ferris wheel seat, but we knew our thinking was selfish. Besides, we loved babies, and the lady was holding a baby, wrapped snugly in a soiled, pink blanket.

"All right," we both answered, and the woman smiled at us.

"I'm Edna Mae," she said.

Well, a smile usually makes most things right, but this smile wasn't the kind you'd feel that way about. Edna Mae was almost pretty, but there was something about the look of her that sent chills down my back.

In the first place, she wasn't clean. There were actually smudges of dirt on her face. Her hair was a bright red-orange. The thick red mass of it looked as if a long time had gone by since a comb had been passed through those greasy strands.

Her eyes were the most frightening, though. Their expression was so haunting, so fearful, so wild, I was afraid to look into them.

Edna Mae had trouble getting into the car because she was holding the baby so tightly to her. The Carny Man helped her, and Jeanné and I both reached out to grab her elbow when she almost lost her balance climbing in.

As she boarded, she said in a shrill, little-girlish voice, "I want to ride in the middle. I always ride in the middle."

Jeanné and I exchanged secret glances of

disappointment, but there wasn't anything we could do. The Carny Man walked away, shaking his head and shrugging his shoulders. I didn't think he should have let a baby ride the Ferris wheel.

I'll have to admit that wasn't the most fun I'd ever had riding the wheel. Something about that lady unnerved me, and I could see Jeanné felt the same way. For one thing, we couldn't sway the seat at all; we knew that wouldn't be polite with this woman on board, and we were worried about the baby.

When we reached the top the seat swayed slightly on its own, as it usually did. Jeanné and I scarcely moved; we didn't want trouble from the Carny man or this strange woman.

But trouble happened anyway. Edna Mae got scared, and with a sudden violent movement she stood, lifting the steel bar that kept us safe. Her piercing scream sliced through the bright, hot sunlight.

Jeanné and I, at the same moment, reached for her and pulled her back into the seat. But as we did, the baby flew from her arms. Frantic, Jeanné and I grabbed for the baby. In terror we scrambled about. I almost fell, but in a moment we were all seated. In her hands Jeanné held the dirty, pink blanket. In my hands was a rubber, life-sized baby doll.

We were hysterical. Below we could see people

rushing about, looking up at us in our dangerously swaying seat.

We could see the Carny Man frenziedly working on the engine, getting us down. As soon as we reached the bottom he rushed towards us, his face grey with fear and anxiety.

Jeanné and I were both sobbing.

"It's all right," I cried, "it's not a real baby. Oh, thank heavens, it's not a real baby."

Edna Mae's eyes were hostile, her mouth turned down in anger. She snatched the baby from me, tore the blanket from Jeanné's hands, and, with a great show of caring, covered the baby and grasped it to her.

The Carny Man helped Edna Mae out of her seat. She just stood there stroking the doll, snuggling it close to her, and crooning, "There, there. That was a nasty fall, darling, but you're just fine. Not a scratch on you, little sweetie."

We stared at her, still sniffling. Then the Carny Man turned to us, and after making sure we were all right, he said, "Now, y'all take this lady home, you hear? Seem like she got some kinda thinking problem."

Jeanné and I didn't know what to do. We stood looking at the woman with big eyes. We were still in shock. Even knowing the baby was only a doll hadn't calmed us down yet.

"Is your home somewhere around here?" I asked. "Can we help you?"

"Thank you, honey," she said in a polite little-girl voice, "but Miss Tilly will help me. Miss Tilly's my best friend."

She walked away, waving a hand at us and smiling as she called back. "We had a nice time, didn't we?"

A nice time? Jeanné and I looked at each other in disbelief.

"You see?" I said. "That proves it. Miss Tilly is a witch, and either Edna Mae is one, too, or Miss Tilly's cast a spell on her. I mean, it's obvious she's as crazy as a bat."

Jeanné nodded vehemently. "That's for sure," she said. "I bet she's in cahoots with Miss Tilly."

"Did you hear what she said?" I asked. I imitated Edna Mae. "'Miss Tilly's my best friend.' Oh, sure, a *friendly* witch. *Uh huh!*"

At first, I couldn't understand my folks' reaction to what had happened. Oh, they were kind and sympathetic; they realized I had been through a terrible experience. But they told me Edna Mae hadn't been thinking straight for a long time. Her mother, her husband, and a nurse took care of her. The day we met her she had somehow slipped out of the house where they kept her secluded.

Jeanné and I felt sorry for her. We both realized we had heard stories about Edna Mae who was, as some folks said, "crazy as a loon." Jeanné said she'd have a special novena for her at

34

the Catholic church. That very night I started to include poor Edna Mae in my prayers. Even as I prayed, I wondered if it was wrong to think she might be a witch.

Jeanné and I both had nightmares about that day. We couldn't help wondering about Edna Mae and Miss Tilly. "Miss Tilly will help me," she had said.

I didn't dare tell Mama about her saying that. I suppose I should have, but she had become very upset with me the last time I had mentioned Miss Tilly being a witch. I decided I'd better keep these suspicions to myself.

But Jeanné and I talked about it a lot. "I wonder if Miss Tilly put a hex on her?" Jeanné asked.

That simple question was all it took for me to believe that was exactly what had happened.

I nodded. "I definitely think she's been turned into a witch and is under some kind of horrible spell."

But then . . . happy days of No-More-Homework and months of summer vacation stretched before us. For a while we forgot Miss Tilly, witches, haunted houses, and ghosts. For a while.

When the Cat's Away ...

O ne day in mid July Papa brought a hobo up from the shop, just when Mama was baking an angel food cake to take with her to the church for some meeting.

Often homeless men would catch rides on the supply train that came down from Mobile three times a week. These homeless men (we called them hobos) would go from house to house, begging food. Sometimes Papa would bring one of these hobos up to the house and ask Mama to give him a meal.

Mama was a little upset that Papa had brought the man up when she was busy, but she felt sorry for the fellow. She scrounged around to find something for him. We had eaten our dinner at noon. That was our big meal. There'd be a long while before she'd be fixing supper. But Papa could always depend on Mama's good heart, despite her fussing.

I usually liked these men. They were friendly and eager to talk, even with a child. And they were grateful to Papa and Mama. I loved to sit at the table on the back porch where they ate. I'd lean forward, my arms folded on the table, listening breathlessly to their exciting hobo tales.

But this man had mean, bloodshot eyes. This man had two yellow eye teeth that grew long, almost over his lips. This man had dark blonde hair that was as scraggly as it was dirty.

I'd have forgiven him for that. Maybe he couldn't help the way he looked, but he wasn't friendly at all.

He had terrible manners. He ate the soup Mama prepared for him with noisy slurps. He didn't close his mouth when he ate, either. He was disgusting.

But I tried to be nice to him.

"Have you been to Bayou La Batre before?" I asked.

He grunted, "Yeah."

I tried again. "Did you ever eat dinner with any other families?"

"Yeah," he mumbled.

Well, he certainly doesn't tell you much, I thought.

"Um . . . uh . . . who?" I asked, hoping Mama

37

wasn't listening. She'd scold me for asking so many questions. She didn't like me being nosy.

Obviously he thought I was rude, but he didn't have to act so rude himself. After all, he was the one who started the rudeness.

He glared at me and sighed, "Um, uh, Tilly something. Big house. Over t'other side of the bayou."

He took a bite of biscuit. The crumbs blew out when he talked.

As disgusted as I was at his eating manners I was excited to hear about his knowing Miss Tilly.

My voice was shrill when I asked him, "You know Miss Tilly?"

He nodded, took a slurp of soup, and ignored me.

I knew it. This was a mean, impolite man, dirty and evil looking. And those teeth surely meant he was a *vampire*. That's it! He was a vampire!

When I went into the house and whispered this to Mama, she was more than a little annoyed. She said, "I don't wanna hear anything about such a silly thing. For goodness sakes, let the man eat! Can't you see he's hungry? Stop annoying the poor fella."

I don't know why she couldn't understand. He wasn't even polite to her, even after she had gone to all that trouble. Money was scarce at our house during the Depression, too. I said that to her.

She stopped whatever she was doing and put her hands on my shoulders. "Marcie," she said, "I don't ever want you to talk that way again. God has blessed us more than most, and if we can't share with others, we might as well not be alive."

I was ashamed I'd mentioned that. I knew we were blessed. My mama knew how to make a lot from a little, and she and Papa were always ready to give to people who were in need of anything. Yet I wondered if she knew how dangerous this man might be. Couldn't she see the way he didn't smile or thank her? He wasn't grateful at all. But what else can you expect from a vampire?

The next day Lena came to help Mama with the washing and ironing, and Mama asked her to look after me.

Everyone was gone. Raymie was out shrimping with the Ledux's on their boat, the *Silver Swan*. He'd be gone a week, most likely. Papa had gone over to Pascagoula, Mississippi, on business for the hardware shop. Mama was going to be busy at the church all day. She was helping the women cook gumbo for the church supper. Mr. Jake was busy; Papa had asked him to mind the shop while he was away.

Usually Lena was nice about talking with me, but before Mama left for church she made a point of asking me not to bother her.

"All that talk can drive a person crazy," she said.

So I was bored.

I drew pictures and colored them with the crayons from the giant pencil box Mama'd bought in Mobile the last time she was there.

I read two and a half *Bobbsey Twins* books; I'd read both of them last year.

I ate leftover pot likker from the turnip greens we'd had for dinner the night before. Pot likker is what we called the juice, or au jus, from the greens. I heated it and poured it over a big slice of corn bread. I *loved* pot likker and corn bread.

I spread two pieces of bread with Mama's extra sweet fig preserves and carefully covered every inch of the bread with pecan halves.

I drank three glasses of iced tea with two teaspoons of sugar stirred in each glass.

I got sick.

After I threw up I was so weak that I went to sleep. I awakened hot with perspiration. The electric fan blew me dry, and I remembered again how bored I was. Lying there, half-dreaming, a golden idea came to me.

I cranked the handle on the phone hanging on the wall of our back porch. In long, drawn-out vowels and crisp consonants Miss Euphonia at the telephone company said, "Bayou Telephone. May I help you?"

I said, "Miss Euphonia, this is Marcie Delchamps. Will you get Jeanné for me?"

She said she would, but first she said, "Now

40

don't you two girls tie up the lines too long. It isn't polite, and you never know when there might be some incorrible catastrophe."

She always said that.

When I was six I asked Mama what "incorrible catastrophe" meant. She laughed until there were tears in her eyes.

"I think she means someone may get hurt in a bad accident and have to call the doctor."

"Incorrible catastrophe" worked; we kept our calls short.

"Whaddaya doing?" I asked Jeanné.

"Nothing," she said.

"Me neither," I said. "Wanna do something?"

"Like what?" she asked, sounding as bored as I felt.

"C'mon over. I'll think of something."

When I hung up the phone I sat down on the front porch swing to wait for Jeanné. As I softly moved back and forth in the swing, I wondered, *What could we do that would be really, really exciting? Really thrilling? Different?*

Mama had a saying about the trouble children get into when their parents aren't around.

"When the cat's away, the mice will play," she'd say.

Well, I'm not comparing my mama or my papa to cats. But I suppose I sort of acted like a mouse.

I'm a little bit ashamed to say what I thought of doing. Come to think of it, I'm a *lot* ashamed.

After all, Mama and Papa had specifically said we shouldn't trespass on anyone's property. Especially Miss Tilly's.

I didn't set out to do it. Well, I may have thought of it a tiny bit. But mostly, I thought it would be fun to go visit Pierre. Maybe it was Pierre's fault . . . for not being home.

We sat on his porch steps for a while, drawing circles in the dirt with our toes. Usually Jeanné and I could think of a million things to do. But this was a hot day, and especially humid. The perspiration rolled down our noses and dropped into splats in the dirt.

Every so often we stole glances in the direction of Miss Tilly's house. Jeanné and I talked about the vampire who had eaten at our house.

"Are you sure he was a vampire?" she asked.

"Course," I answered. After I made such a definite answer I knew I'd have to stick by it.

"I dunno, Marcie," Jeanné said, staring at me with those big, blue eyes. "It isn't that I don't believe you, 'cause you know I do, but it's just that you always seem to see things I don't."

"Well, Jeanné," I said, feeling wise, "I don't think you keep your eyes open the way you should."

I thought about what Mama had said and added, "That's 'cause you're prosaic."

I hadn't found out what that word meant, but I trusted Mama.

Confused, Jeanné said, "Maybe."

But then she actually asked me, "You're really sure you saw ghosts' arms that day we were here?"

"Oh, yes," I answered. I was reasonably sure.

"What were the arms doing?" she asked. "How many arms were there?"

I was annoyed with her for putting me on the spot that way.

"Honestly, Jeanné," I said, "surely you didn't expect me to count them, so naturally, I don't know."

I stood up, putting an end to all these uncomfortable questions.

"You know something," I said, "we can't hurt anything if we climb up on the side of her house. We'll be careful not to cause any damage or anything, and we won't even think of going in. Just a quick peek, and then we can jump down."

Jeanné reminded me that Mama had told us not to go in Miss Tilly's backyard again.

I quickly said, "Oh, we won't go in the backyard. We'll climb up to her side balcony and just take a quick peek at the room where we saw the ghosts."

Even as I spoke I knew I was planning a "sneaky deception." That's what Jeanné and I called it when people would hide a wrong thing they had done. But I pushed my guilt so far back in my mind that I couldn't find it after a few moments.

It didn't take much to convince Jeanné, either. We both needed a few lessons in avoiding temptation.

This time we skirted the lot, slipping all the way around it but keeping to the inside. We walked closely behind the bushy, extra tall oleander shrubs that grew along the front of the lot. In the heat the fragrance of the oleander blossoms was strong and sweet.

I was beginning to wish I hadn't said that climbing to that second story balcony would be easy. I wondered how we were going to get there. The roof rose steeply by the window. I hadn't remembered it being that sheer.

I was irritated when Jeanné voiced my fears. "You'll never be able to get up to that window," she said.

That convinced me to try. Of course I could do it. I stood there, studying the possibilities, and an idea came to me.

On the side beneath the window was a tall trellis. A jessamine vine grew thickly to the top of it . . . right by the window. It was covered with sweet-smelling, starlike, white flowers.

I tested the wood. The trellis seemed sturdy.

"We can climb up on this," I said.

"Doesn't look very strong to me," Jeanné said, looking doubtful.

44

"Oh, it is," I said.

Well, maybe it is, I thought. *And besides, we're not very heavy.*

"Wanna go first?" I asked politely.

"No," Jeanné answered sweetly. "I'll let you go first."

I started up.

Right away I began to wonder about the strength of that trellis. I wondered if it was pulling out from the wall. Then I wondered if it might be rotten. Something broke under my right foot, taking my breath away. I quickly went up another step.

I wouldn't look down. I had a slight fear of heights, and feeling that crumbling wood under my foot from this distance didn't help my nerves any.

I reached the window. My eyes were a few inches above the ledge. I peered in, holding my breath.

I could see a bed, a rocking chair, a bureau, and a big, old-fashioned wardrobe chest. Nothing else.

There has to be something more, I thought. *Where are those ghosts' arms?*

At that moment Miss Tilly came into the room, moving slowly, painfully, it seemed, looking older than I remembered. She wasn't looking up, but I didn't want to take any chances. I quickly jerked my head down.

The sudden movement must have been too much for the ancient trellis. It broke. The tumble to the ground took only a second, but I was certain this was the end of my life. My right foot hit first. Hard. There was a sharp, wrenching pain as my ankle twisted. My hands landed flatly on a piece of broken wood from the trellis. I could feel my skin being scraped away.

I blanked out. The last thing I remember was the startled look of horror in Jeanné's bright blue eyes.

A Warlock?

I can't remember the long walk home. Mama said I was probably in shock. She explained how, after an accident, a person's mind sort of closes off, so the pain isn't as bad. She said many times people can't remember the pain or the events that happen immediately afterwards.

But later, there was a greater pain I suffered as I lay in bed with that sprained ankle. Sure, the ankle hurt, but the real pain was guilt pain.

Oh, I explained about climbing on a trellis. I told about the rotten wood. I told about falling.

But I didn't say on whose house that trellis was attached. I suppose she thought I had been over at Jeanné's.

I didn't remember how I had gotten home. Jeanné said she let me lean on her as I hopped all the way down Oak Lane, across Grand Pont, past

48

the drugstore, the barber shop, the five and dime, and all the other little downtown stores.

Jeanné said, "At the bridge I almost fainted 'cause I was so afraid it would open while I was helping you across. Just after I got across, it opened, and I almost got sick to the stomach."

Scolding I asked, "Why didn't you go into Mr. Henson's little room and ask him to be sure we got across? Why, we could've been killed."

I realized then what an ungrateful thing I had said, so I added, "I wanna thank you for helping me home. You probably saved my life."

I was truly thankful, but my memory had to do with arriving home. The hardware shop on the bayou, the big oak with its limbs dipping into the dark, still water, the giant magnolia, our small white house with its green, freshly painted tin roof . . . it had never looked as beautiful.

I didn't mention Sea Trout Lane, or Pierre, or Miss Tilly. The pain I felt was from knowing I was deceiving Mama. I kept trying to convince myself that I wasn't lying—I just wasn't telling the entire story. We hadn't done any harm.

Well, I reasoned, *that ole trellis was so rotten it was gonna crumble up soon. It wasn't worth anything, anyhow.*

Jeanné came to see me, and we whispered as we played with our Sears and Roebuck paper dolls.

"Have you tole your mama?" she asked.

"Not yet," I said, "I don't wanna bother her."

"Your mama would understand," she said. "She's nice about things."

"Yeah, but she already warned me about trespassing on Miss Tilly's property."

"Are you worried it'll make her feel bad?" she asked.

That was the problem. If I had only told her right away. There just didn't seem to be a time when I could tell the truth. When Mama came home from cooking gumbo at the church that day she was tired. She said she'd like to take a nap before going back to the church to serve the supper.

I told her I'd hurt my ankle. She came to the sofa where I was lying and looked at it. She called the doctor right away.

Like I said, when Dr. Ashland came he assured us the ankle wasn't broken . . . just sprained. I didn't like him saying I had to stay off of it.

He smiled and winked at Mama.

"Course I know you'll have a hard time keeping Miss Marcie off her feet. She's so wired up you could use her for an electric generator around here. You could save the money you pay the Alabama Power Company."

He and Mama laughed. Then he turned to me and gave me a kind, but stern look.

"Miss Marcie," he said, "I want you to stay off

that foot, you hear? And I mean it. Miss Helene, could you make a trip to the library and get enough books to keep this young lady sedated?"

The next morning Mama got me six books, but I couldn't read every minute of the day. I had a lot of time to think. I would go over and over the events of that day. I remembered how I had to stay home from the gumbo supper at church that first night. One of the favorite events at our church was the gumbo supper. The ladies made the soup with lots of shrimp and crab meat. They added okras, tomatoes, onions, and spices and served it over big spoonfuls of rice.

After supper they served homemade ice cream. Raymie and the other teenaged boys turned the handles on the freezers, and some of us younger girls would sit on burlap bags that covered the tops.

Jeanné and I noticed how Hank and Raymie would start complaining that we weren't heavy enough, so the teenaged girls would take our places. That made Raymie smile all over his silly face. Especially if Nellie was there.

But the night after my accident Mama said I'd had a big enough day, so I had to stay home. I think that was the first time I ever had to miss a gumbo supper.

I became obsessed with believing I was being punished for not telling Mama the truth. I thought of how Mama often questioned my wild stories, and how she always remarked about my "big imagination." I suppose a person could say I sometimes stretched the truth. But Mama knew I wasn't an out and out liar.

It was Mama's trust in me that had me worried. If I had told her right away it wouldn't have been as difficult. But the longer I kept the truth hidden, the bigger the lie became. That happens.

I don't know how long I would have gone on this way, worrying about how Mama would feel when she knew the truth, but something happened that week that, well . . .

One afternoon I got a call from Jeanné. She asked me to meet her at the drugstore. She said we could buy cherry cokes; her mama had given her a dime for helping out at the café where she worked.

Mama said I could go if I didn't stay too long. We were having a guest for supper—some man who had been a missionary in India. He was the speaker for the Women's Missionary Union's retreat, and he was going to stay with us for a few days.

"I'll be back soon, Mama," I promised.

I hobbled down the street to the drugstore. I was still limping some, but Dr. Ashland had told Mama I needed to exercise the ankle.

Jeanné and I sat at one of the small, white, wrought iron tables and sipped our cokes as slowly as we could. We didn't get many nickles for Coca Colas, so when we did we made them last as long as possible. We'd suck on the straws until they made that slurping noise we called the "drugstore blues."

As we were sitting there the ugliest man we'd ever seen came into the store. He asked the druggist for directions to someone's house.

We remembered how ugly we'd thought Jake had been the first time we saw him. But when Mr. Jake had gotten some clean clothes, when his scraggly hair had been washed and combed, we could see we'd been mistaken.

But this man was spotless in the way he was dressed. He wore a clean, pressed suit, even though the weather was hot and sticky. His black hair was parted and slicked down, and his black shoes shone as brightly as his hair. But his skin was red and mottled, almost like a lizard's skin; we'd never seen skin like that.

"Isn't he scary looking?" I asked Jeanné.

"Really awful," she agreed.

"You know what I think?" I whispered. "I'll just bet you anything that man is a *warlock*."

"What's a warlock?" she asked.

I wasn't sure, but I knew the word meant someone evil. This man looked plenty evil to me.

"You'll have to look it up," I said smugly.

Well, that's what my teacher said when *she* wasn't sure.

I added, "I think it means someone really evil and bad."

"I think so, too," Jeanné agreed. "Maybe he's come to town to visit Miss Tilly."

You can just about imagine how shocked I felt when I walked into our living room a half hour later and saw that warlock sitting there, talking to Mama.

"Marcie, honey," Mama said, "this is Brother Saul. You know, our guest I was telling you about?"

I was horrified. When we were alone in the kitchen, fixing supper, I asked her if she had ever met this Brother Saul before.

"Well, no, but I've heard about him for years. He's such a wonderful man."

"Mama," I said, "you should call and have someone send you a picture of that missionary. This man is probably impersonating him. You've heard 'bout people doing that on the radio, haven't you?"

Mama groaned and looked toward the ceiling.

"Marcie," she said, "sometimes I can't understand you whatsoever. You are really a very suspicious little girl. Why, you'd think you'd experienced all sorts of horrors in your life. Where do you get such ideas?"

I could see she wasn't happy with me, so I didn't say any more. But I told Raymie as soon as I had the chance. He agreed with me when he ran into Brother Saul in the hall accidentally that night. He had jumped and hollered.

Brother Saul laughed and excused himself.

"It's funny how startled we get when we aren't expecting someone, isn't it?" he'd said.

Yeah, I thought, *someone like a warlock.*

He was with Mama at the retreat all day Friday. I was worried about her, and I was really glad when she got home in the afternoon.

Mama and Papa listened to his every word. I could see they were really taken by his charming ways, but I felt he had a scary way of snooping around.

After breakfast was over on Saturday morning, and Mama had gone with Brother Saul to the retreat, I went down to see Raymie. He was sweeping the wharf at the hardware store.

The sky was the brightest of blues, the clouds so thick and white I knew if I could get up there I'd be able to curl up on one. Everything was so beautiful I almost forgot witches, vampires, and ghosts.

But not warlocks.

"Whaddaya think of Brother Saul?" I asked. "Isn't he weird?"

"Sure is," Raymie said. "Whooh! Did you ever see such an ugly man?"

"I know," I giggled. "I think he wears a wig."

"That's a toupee," Raymie corrected me.

"Whatever," I said. "Isn't his skin awful? Sort

of speckled looking. You know what he looks like? Other than a warlock? A big, giant beetle."

I loved it when Raymie laughed at my descriptions. His knees got so weak he had to sit down on the wharf to keep from falling in the bayou.

"More like a grasshopper," he wheezed through hysterical laughter.

"Maybe a praying mantis," I cried, as weak from laughter as he.

I was thinking of how tall and skinny the man was, and how long his arms had looked when he folded his hands in prayer at the supper table.

"But anyone that ugly has to be a warlock," I said, gasping.

"What's a warlock?" Raymie asked.

"You'll have to look it up," I said.

I had been intending to do that myself when I had a chance.

We didn't notice Papa come up to us. He had been coiling rope on the other side of the gas pumps. He walked over to us, and the look in his eyes told us he wasn't happy.

My papa scarcely ever lost his temper. He had a reputation for being the most even-tempered man in Mobile county, and he deserved it. He was only angry when a person was treated unfairly. Mama called that "righteous indignation."

He stood staring at us, his arms folded. I always thought of his blue eyes twinkling, but there wasn't a twinkle in them now. They didn't even look blue; anger seemed to have changed them to a steely grey. His voice was steely, too.

"Raymie. There's work to be done inside the shop. Get on in there. Marcie. Go up to your room and stay there until supper."

"What'd we do?" Raymie whined, and I, too, stared at Papa in bewilderment.

"I will not tolerate my children making fun of their fellow man."

He had heard us talking about Brother Saul. Raymie turned and walked into the shop.

I tried to put my arm around Papa's waist, but he took my hand away. There was nothing that hurt more than being rejected by my papa.

"Do as I say, young lady," he said. There was no answering warmth in his face.

"Yes, sir," I said, and I turned to walk down the slanting wharf planks to the ground. I felt terrible. The crushed oyster shells of the road were harsh on my bare feet, and the sky was bright and glaring now.

Papa and Raymie didn't come up to the house until it was time for supper. Raymie went to the kitchen to wash his hands while Papa went to the bathroom to wash his.

Brother Saul was in the bedroom getting ready. Mama was out picking a bouquet of lavender cosmos to put on the table.

I whispered to Raymie, "What'd he say?"

Raymie shook his head, confused. "Nothing."

"Nothing?" I couldn't believe this.

"He scarcely said a word to me all afternoon."

I had seldom seen Raymie this troubled.

"We weren't doing anything," Raymie said, "just laughing a little. Why, even Papa will have to admit, the man *is* funny looking."

I agreed. "It's obvious he's fooled Papa as bad as he's fooled Mama. I just know he's a warlock."

"Nah, I think you're probably wrong 'bout that. But he *is* scary looking."

Brother Saul was with us three days. I'll have to admit he sort of grew on us. He smiled a lot, he was thoughtful to Mama, and he had interesting things to tell us about India.

The morning after he left, Papa came up to the house for lunch. He handed Raymie and me a clipping from the *Mobile Press Register* from a long time ago.

"Read it!" he said, and we knew this was a command.

The article was about a boy who had run into a burning house on Government Street in Mobile. He'd saved an entire family, but the boy was so badly burned they had to send him somewhere up north to a special hospital for burned people. He never looked the same again.

That boy's name was Saul Averell.

Our Brother Saul.

I didn't change my mind about Miss Tilly, or the ghosts and vampires. But when I read that story, I began to love Brother Saul. It filled me with love, and caring, and sweetness. And shame. I couldn't hold back the tears.

I saw tears in Raymie's eyes, too. That really hurt. Raymie never cried.

"Oh, Papa," I cried out. I couldn't stop the tears.

Mama came over to me. She put her arms around me and hugged. Papa said, "I thought you had learned about judging people when you were so afraid of Jake."

"I know, I know," I sobbed. I turned back to Mama's comforting arms. "Oh, Mama, Mama."

All the guilt I had been feeling for deceiving her came pouring out.

"Mama," I said, my voice weak, "I've been lying about something I did."

"What? What are you talking about, Marcie?"

I snivelled, trying to stop crying so I could tell her. And I did. I told how I had talked Jeanné into going with me to Miss Tilly's. I told about climbing and breaking the trellis.

"But the worst thing, Mama, I kept lying to you, and I'm being punished for it. For instance, I sprained my ankle. And I couldn't go to the gumbo supper, and oh, just a lot of little things have been happening to me," I wailed. "See? I'm being punished."

Mama calmed me down. "You're not being punished." She smiled. "It's only natural you'd fall

59

when you're on a rotten trellis. And, of course, your foot will probably be sprained when you land from ten or twelve feet."

"I suppose I was involved in what Miss Euphonia would call an 'incorrible catastrophe,' huh?"

Papa's eyes crinkled at the corners. He liked that.

But then, the smile gone from her face, the black eyes serious, Mama said, "You did right to confess, Marcie, but there is something now that you must do."

Sobered, I said, "What? I'll do whatever you say."

"You must take some money out of your bank and pay someone to make a new trellis for Miss Tilly."

My heart felt as if it dropped to my toes. I'd been saving that money for a doll trunk.

I said, "Yes, Ma'am."

"And you must go visit Miss Tilly. You need to apologize to her."

"No!" I cried, "I can't do that. I won't do that!"

"Whatever happened to doing whatever Mama says?" Papa asked.

"Papa," I wailed, "you know all us kids are scared of Miss Tilly."

It's one thing to play at being a Peeping Tom, looking in a witch's window, but to go visit her?

My mama wasn't an easy person to talk out of something she believed. And she was absolutely certain she was doing the honorable-parent thing by having me apologize.

Apologizing to Miss Tilly

O n Saturday afternoon Mama had me dress in my yellow organdy Sunday dress with the blue satin sash. She insisted I wear a matching bow on top of my straight Buster Brown haircut. I thought I looked ridiculous. I hoped none of my friends would see me.

When I complained about wearing a stiff organdy dress on such a hot day, Mama said, "I know, darling, but Miss Tilly will just love it. She used to have a little girl herself, many years ago. Her daughter, I believe her name was Ruthanne, was a young woman, only twenty-five, when she died. Miss Tilly misses her still."

I knew what Mama was doing . . . trying to make me feel sorry for the old woman. I guess she figured if I felt sorry enough I wouldn't have any room left for being afraid. Well, I was sorry for her. But I was afraid, too.

"And you should take her some goodies," Mama said, rummaging in her pantry shelves for scuppernong jam, fig preserves, and blackberry jam.

"And here are some of last year's pecans," she added. "They keep nicely."

"I can't carry all that," I protested.

She was firm. "Of course you can. Here. This basket will hold everything." She handed me a small, white, straw basket. Then she cocked her head to the side, thinking.

"Ah, yes!" she said as she broke off a gladiola blossom from the vase on the kitchen table. She tied it on the basket handle with a pink ribbon.

"Now, isn't that pretty?" she asked, pleased with herself.

"Yes'm."

I was miserable. My head was aching . . . not with just a dull throb, but with a pounding, thudding ache.

"Mama, I better not go," I said. "I have a terrible headache, and I feel like I'm gonna be sick to the stomach."

She shook her head. Sadly, I thought.

"Ah, Marcie, I can't believe you'd pull this kind of trick on me. You're just trying to keep from going. Now, you just pull yourself together."

I could understand what she was thinking,

but I couldn't understand why I felt this bad. I was miserably afraid, but I truly felt ill.

I suppose there were several reasons. Not only was I scared to death of Miss Tilly. I was dressed for Sunday school on a hot Saturday afternoon when I'd usually be wearing shorts and halters. I would be swinging a fancy basket on my arm like Little Red Riding Hood. And I would have to admit to that old lady I had trespassed on her property.

I felt hotter than the day itself.

"I think I have a fever," I grumbled to myself. I truly believed I did. I wanted to ask Mama to take my temperature, but I knew she was convinced I was thinking of an excuse to stay home.

I felt as if I were going to cry.

"Couldn't Jeanné go with me? Just halfway, maybe?"

"Absolutely not," she said, giving a short, negative shake with her head. I knew that shake. It meant *no.*

How would she like to walk across the bayou on a hot August afternoon? I thought. I was immediately sorry. I knew I was doing the right thing, even though all the bones, muscles, and skin of my body were fighting against it.

But I had to take one last chance.

"Mama," I said, "do you know about Miss Tilly putting a hex on Mr. Jake?"

Mama frowned. "I certainly hope you're not

going to bring up that foolish notion about her being a witch again."

"Did you notice how Mr. Jake had his arm in a sling for a while?"

"He had a fall," Mama said, pressing her lips together firmly.

I persisted. I told her what Pierre had told me. I tried to make the story as dramatic as Pierre had.

"You remember one day Mr. Jake went over to Sea Trout Lane to deliver a message from Papa to Mr. Martin?"

She continued to press her lips together in that maddening way she had when she'd made up her mind in advance that she didn't want to hear what I was saying.

However, she opened those tightened lips enough to say, "Yes, I remember."

"Well!" I said, taking center stage in the living room, "Mr. Jake was passing by Miss Tilly's house. She came out on the porch, waving her hands at him wildly, in a weird and crazy way."

I waited. Mama said nothing. For a moment I actually felt I was going to faint. "Well," I said, "Mr. Jake thinks everybody is as nice as he is, so he went over to her, smiling that sweet, trusting smile of his. Pierre was worried, naturally. He could see she was up to no good.

"Suddenly," I continued, my voice getting really dramatic, "Miss Tilly raised her hands in

65

the air and *shouted* something, really loud, Mama."

Mama's curiosity got the better of her, and she said, "Did Pierre say what she yelled?"

"No, Ma'am," I had to admit, "but Pierre said he knows it was some sort of incantation."

"Marcie!" Mama exclaimed.

"But don't you see?" I said, warming to the most important part of the story. "That's when Mr. Jake fell and sprained his arm."

"That's ridiculous," Mama said, really angry now. "You and Pierre are letting your imaginations get the better of you. Now, you listen to me. Miss Tilly is a harmless, sweet old lady. She is *not* a witch."

Poor Mama, I thought. *That ole lady has her fooled.*

There was no use arguing, but I was feeling more ill all the time. I said, "Mama, I feel really sick and my head hurts really bad."

Mama lost her patience at that.

"If you think you're going to get my sympathy and change my mind about your going, you're wrong." And with that, she put her hand on my bottom and pushed me out the door.

As I trudged over Grand Pont, down Oak Tree Road, and made the turn onto Sea Trout Lane, I thought about a lot of things. I was sorry for myself. I really did feel sick . . . all over.

And I thought about Miss Tilly. I knew she

couldn't help being old. Ninety-six, some people said. And I knew she couldn't help the way she walked, moving sideways, like a crab. I wasn't sure about her teeth; why hadn't she done something about them?

The day was hot. I mean, really hot. I felt the warmth all through me, in my flesh, my bones, and my skin. But strange little chills kept running up and down my arms.

As I walked down Sea Trout Lane I thought I saw something. The vampire hobo! Just behind that tree up ahead. I walked real slow, watching. No, he wasn't there. Then I spotted him again—in a stand of oak trees up ahead. He didn't look solid like a real flesh-and-blood person. His body was a shimmering, blurry mass. I blinked my eyes. Was he really there, or was I imagining it?

The sun was shining with a bright hotness as I neared the house. My dress was wet with perspiration, but I was beginning to feel cold. Really cold. I couldn't understand why I felt cold on such a hot day. Maybe I was having double chills from the thought of meeting those ghosts.

I was trembling as I arrived at the house. At the gate I stopped and stared at the house. The greyed, wooden shape of it was dark and still, haunted-looking even in the sharp sunshine. The windows were cruel and curious eyes.

Is she standing behind one of them, staring out at me with those sunken eyes?

I straightened my shoulders and lifted my chin. The effort hurt my head.

The gladiola was coming loose from the bow Mama had tied. I set the basket down to tighten the pink ribbon. I took a deep, uneven breath and lifted the basket again. My arms were weak; the basket felt heavy.

I didn't know what was wrong with me. I couldn't seem to think straight. Perhaps Miss Tilly had already put a hex on me.

There was no turning back now. I walked up the worn, creaky steps. My hand didn't want to obey, but I finally knocked at the door. Timidly. Then, more boldly. There was no answer.

I was ready to say a thank-you prayer when the door creaked open. The long, bony face of Miss Tilly peered out at me. Her face was as wrinkled as I remembered. Her nose was as long. Her hair was as greasy and scraggly. And her eyes . . . her eyes were as dark-circled and haunting as a *witch's!*

Chills rippled down my back and behind my knees, making me more weak than ever. I held the basket to her, extended away from my body as far as possible. My squeaky voice seemed to belong to someone else.

"Miss Tilly, I'm Marcie Delchamps, and my mama sent me with a few little gifts, and . . . I'm the one who broke your trellis, and . . . I . . . I'm sorry."

I expelled a long, quavering breath.

For what seemed like ninety-eight years she stared at me. Her smile didn't make me feel any better. Closed lips pulled up at both corners of her mouth in a silly grin.

"My trellis is broken?" she asked in a shaky, scratchy voice.

Oh, no. Don't tell me she doesn't even know? Why, I didn't need to tell her.

Right away I was ashamed of that thought. I straightened my shoulders and lifted my chin again.

"Yes, Ma'am," I quavered. "I . . . I sort of . . . climbed on it, but I didn't mean to break it, and I'm going to use my money to have a new one built for you."

"Well!" she said, taking the basket. "Aren't you a nice little girl? Miss Helene's little girl, aren't you? What a kind lady. Why, maybe she could send that nice Mr. Jake to fix it."

There, I thought, *Mama ought to hear this. Already she's planning to put another spell on poor Mr. Jake.*

Then Miss Tilly said, "Come on in, dear."

In a whispery rush I said, "Uh, no, Ma'am. You see, I have to get back . . . as soon as . . . possible."

I smiled, a great big false smile. I wasn't prepared for what she did then. A long, bony hand reached out and grasped my arm and pulled me into the hallway.

"Nonsense," she gummed, her lips tight over where the teeth used to be. "I want you to come in and let me get to know you better."

My weak knees could scarcely hold up as I stepped into that dark, eerie house.

The Invisible Maid

A s Miss Tilly led me down the hall, the chills behind my knees continued to ripple up and down, and there were other chills, too, down my spine and on my arms and legs.

Miss Tilly limped along, sort of sideways, like a crab. Once she turned to smile at me. "I'm so happy you came, Ruthanne," she said.

Ruthanne? She thought I was her dead daughter! What if she was crazy, like that Edna Mae at the carnival?

The living room convinced me the place was haunted. The furniture was old and large. There were cobwebs in the corners of the room. The heavy brocaded drapes were closed, and the sofa and armchairs were covered with dusty sheeting.

Miss Tilly peered into the basket. "Your mother is a gracious lady," she said. "How dear of her to

71

send me goodies from her kitchen. Preserves. Mmmmm. She seems to know what it's like to be old and forgotten, doesn't she?"

I was thinking maybe she wasn't a witch, after all, but then she looked up at me, and she actually cackled. "Oh, we're going to have a marvelous time together, aren't we, honey? I just *love* little girls."

She set the basket on a table and led me to the sofa. "Now, you just sit right here, honey," she said, and sat right down beside me. I thought I was going to faint. My head was pounding, and the room became blurred. I blinked to clear my eyes.

Miss Tilly stroked my arm with her bony fingers. Mama had taught me to be polite, and I knew that meant even in a room that was dark, dusty, and damp, and even with someone I didn't like. I tried to muster a sincere smile.

I said, "Miss Tilly, I really need to go."

She just ignored me. "We'll have a nice, long visit, honey," she said. She patted me. I have never liked being patted. It makes me feel about three years old.

"Yes, Ma'am," I answered, "but you know I can't stay."

She said, "*Nonsense*." I'd never heard anyone say that word with such emphasis. She stood up and turned that weird smile on me full force.

"My goodness!" she said. "Where have my

manners gone? You'd like some refreshments, wouldn't you, honey?"

That was a horrible thought. Refreshments meant the time it would take to prepare them. As politely as I possibly could, I answered, "Uh, no, Ma'am. I really do need to get home, but thank you so much."

"*Nonsense!*" she said.

She was unsteady for a moment, but she regained her balance and walked slowly to a corner of the room. I turned to look. I didn't want to take my eyes off of her.

An ancient bell cord hung from the ceiling. I'd read in books that this was the way people used to summon their servants. When the cord was pulled a bell would sound in other parts of the house to let the servants know their mistress wanted something.

I stared at the rope. At the end of it a sinister red dragon was embroidered on a black damask panel fringed with red. Yellow tongues of fire were spewing from its mouth.

Of course, I thought, *that's exactly what a witch would have. But what could she be doing? She doesn't have any servants.*

The gnarled, old hands pulled the rope with some effort. She had to be completely out of her mind. Hadn't she called me Ruthanne when I first came? And now she was thinking she had servants!

Slowly and painfully she returned to the sofa. Slowly and painfully she sat beside me again. Each movement was in slow motion. I didn't like the way she watched the door. Expectantly. Smiling. I felt worse than ever.

What? Who is she expecting?

Then into the room there came . . . now, this may be difficult to believe, but into the room there came . . . an *apron*. That's right. A small, white, starched, cotton apron. Ruffled. And just about where a head should be, a white, ruffled maid's cap.

No head.

No body.

Nobody?

This thing, this *it*, carried a large silver tray, and on this tray was a delicate china tea pot. China cups and saucers, too. And a matching plate filled with petit fours and pound cake. I'd only seen petit fours at a fancy wedding my family had attended in Mobile once. They were small, square cakes, pastel colored and iced with decorative ribbons and flowers.

It . . . she set the cake down on the low table before us. Then the white apron and cap left the room. I stared after it, rubbing my eyes, unbelieving. For some reason, even Miss Tilly was beginning to seem blurred and shadowy.

Something's terribly wrong with me, I thought. *I have really been hexed.*

Miss Tilly leaned forward, picked up the teapot with trembling hands, and poured.

"Have a little tea, honey," she offered.

"No, thank you, Ma'am," I said, but she ignored me. She must have been a little deaf.

My hands trembled, too, as I took a sip of tea. *Why, it's real tea*, I thought. *A ghost brought real tea!*

Then I noticed the tea set. Mama didn't have many pretty things; she would have loved having a tea set like this. It was the most beautiful thing I had seen in my entire ten years. I could almost see through the delicate china, hand-painted with pink and purple roses and pale green leaves.

"That is the prettiest tea set I have ever seen in my whole, long life," I said.

Miss Tilly was delighted. "Oh, what a sweet thing to say!" she exclaimed.

I would have loved a glass of Coca Cola with ice to soothe my parched throat. But tea was better than nothing. Trembling as I was, I somehow got the cup to my lips a second time without spilling any of it. To my surprise, the tea tasted good . . . sort of sweet and minty.

She watched me intently, every move I made. As soon as I swallowed she insisted, "Have some dessert, Ruthanne."

Ruthanne again! I looked at her, but she just pointed at the cakes.

I wasn't hungry, but I wanted to taste those

sweets. My hands continued to tremble. I dropped two petit fours before I could pick one up. I was surprised at how good they tasted, despite my queasy stomach.

Miss Tilly giggled, the way a young girl does. "You look so pretty, my dear, in that lovely yellow dress. Little girls should never wear those horrid shorts and halters. So unbecoming."

Well, Mama had evidently been right about what I should wear. I thought of how I had begged Mama to let me wear my shorts and halter.

Miss Tilly gummed a piece of cake. I tried not to look. My queasy stomach was getting worse by the moment. My lips were dry, but moisture welled up in my throat, the way it does when you are nauseated. I kept swallowing to keep from throwing up.

I began to wonder what the desserts had in them. The illustration from one of my fairy tale books came to me. The witch was pushing Hansel into the oven.

Will I come out as pound cake or petit four? I wondered.

But after a while my stomach calmed down. I almost convinced myself there was nothing more to fear. Maybe that invisible maid was just a "figment of my imagination," as Papa said.

But just then Miss Tilly pushed herself up and said, "Oh, my gracious, honey, you must be getting bored. Well, I know just how we can fix that."

She moved across the room toward the bell cord.

"You love music, don't you, Ruthanne?"

Ruthanne again. Why couldn't she remember my name? This was crazy.

The feeble hands grasped the cord and pulled. What was going to happen next?

The Ghostly Pianist

After she pulled the cord she returned to the sofa again to sit beside me, panting as she lowered herself into the seat.

"There!" she exclaimed with a triumphant croak, "I just know you're going to love this. Miss Evelyn is *so* talented."

As we sipped our tea I stole quick glances at the door, looking for the person who would answer the bell summons. I hoped that Miss Evelyn would have a body.

And then I saw . . . *it*. A pale green scarf fluttering in the breeze, tied around an invisible neck. Gloves filled with invisible fingers, swinging at thigh height. I could hear the staccato sound of high heels crossing the room, and someone passed by me.

Across the room stood a big, black upright

piano. And there she . . . *it* . . . removed the gloves and carefully placed them on the top of the piano.

The keys began to move. Someone was playing a Chopin waltz my piano teacher had tried to teach me.

Mama would have called this music a "work of art." To me it was the work of one of those specters that Mama and Papa said didn't exist.

Just you wait till I tell them, I thought. *They'll be sorry they didn't listen to me.*

Miss Tilly said, "Now, isn't that divine? Don't you just love it?"

"Yes, Ma'am," I assured her. The music was beautiful, but I was truly beginning to be ill now. The pounding in my head had increased; I could hear the loud thump of my heart with each beat. With the palm of my hand I felt my forehead. I was surprised at the hotness of my skin. I wondered if fear had made me sick.

"Ruthanne used to love playing that piece," Miss Tilly said.

As nice as the music was, I thought Miss Evelyn was never going to stop. I mean, if a person ever heard and saw a *nothing* playing a piano, she'd know what I mean.

My hands were cold.

My knees were weak.

My heart was faint.

My spine was jelly.

As I looked about the room my vision blurred;

there were two of every object. Overcome with dizziness, I fell over onto the couch.

Miss Tilly made an odd sound and stood up. She bent over me, her voice muffled and faint as if she were far away. "Everything's going to be all right, honey," she said.

Yeah, I thought, *all right for you. Now you have me just where you want me. I know what happens when you pull that bell cord.*

Would I ever get out of here alive?

The Basement

T rue to my terrifying thoughts, the next thing that came into the room was a great, big, *really* big suit of coveralls. The striped blue-and-white ticking kind with the brass clip adjusters on the shoulders.

As usual, no body.

No head.

No feet.

No arms.

Nobody.

I figured if there were a body beneath that overall it would probably weigh three hundred pounds. The overall looked and moved as if it covered a lot of flesh.

It . . . he . . . panted as he moved toward me in the way a heavy person would.

A husky voice asked, "Where shall I put her?"

Oh, oh, oh, my thoughts wailed, *what are they going to do with me?*

"Oh, dear, let me see," Miss Tilly said. "Why don't you take her down to the basement, Jean. It's cooler down there."

She pronounced Jean in the French way. *Jawn.*

The word *cooler* caused the goose pimples to rise again. I was sure she wanted to keep me cool so I wouldn't "spoil." Mama put shrimp in the ice box so they would "keep" before she cooked them.

As I lay there, not knowing whether I was awake or asleep, Jean padded over to the sofa. His big overall form stood over me. He must have stooped then, because what felt like big hands slid under me and lifted me up. I could feel the rough texture of heavy denim on my arms and legs.

He carried me to the hall and then, with Miss Tilly following closely behind, we went down the dark, narrow stairs to the basement.

The dust rose from a big, overstuffed couch as he placed me there. The living room had seemed dreadful, but the basement was horrible. This long room was darker, drearier, more damp and depressing than anything I'd ever seen.

"We'll be back, honey," Miss Tilly said, hovering over me. "Just you sleep for a while. Don't you worry about anything, you sweet child."

Sweet? Like sugar? Like gingerbread men? Like pound cake?

83

She and Jean went back up the stairs, leaving me to wonder what they had planned for me.

My eyes surveyed my surroundings. The basement was cluttered with old chairs, tables, paintings, an ancient rocking horse, a dressmaker form draped in old, yellowed lace, and many other items. Everything was old and smelled of mold.

I tried to get up, but I was too weak. I fell back, exhausted from the effort.

For a while I was left alone. Once Miss Tilly brought a kerosene lamp and set it on a table nearby. She stroked my face, then silently went up the stairs.

I looked wildly about. There was a row of small windows above my head, too high for me to reach. The one door leading outside had a large chifforobe in front of it; I'd never be able to move that. The only other exit was the opening to the narrow, darkened stairs leading to Miss Tilly and her evil spirits. I couldn't take that route.

The tears I had held back finally came. There was something about being unable to move, to scream, to speak clearly. I knew I was very, very sick. Maybe I was sick because of the fear, but I was definitely sick.

Papa said when you're in a dangerous situation you should take one step at a time. But what could you do when you didn't even have the strength to move?

A Human Ball

Miss Tilly came down the stairs to check on me. She carried a basin filled with cold water. When she tried to wash my face I pulled away from her. I knew Mama wouldn't like how rude I was, but I didn't want my face washed.

She said, "Now, honey, hold still and let Miss Tilly wash your little face."

She was preparing me for something. I had a mental vision of Mama washing a chicken before she baked it. I kept my face turned away, and eventually she left.

Relieved, I curled myself into a tight, round ball by circling my arms with my knees.

Then, suddenly, the strangest creatures of all bounded into the room. There were two of them, and they were a dark, ugly green. Long hair covered their short, stocky bodies.

They emerged from opposite corners of the basement, chortling with glee. Their good nature was frightening; they grinned constantly in a crazed, wild manner.

In a shrill voice one of them cried out, "Wanna play a game of catch, Pitooey?"

I thought maybe he was talking to me, but the second one answered in gruff and gravelly tones, "Sure, Phooey, why not?"

Pitooey came toward me, rubbing his hairy hands together gleefully.

"Sure," he cackled, "Why not? She's just the right weight. Skinny and bony."

Pitooey lifted me with arms as strong as Jean's. He actually threw me across the room to Phooey as if I weighed no more than a rubber ball. Terrified, I kept my arms tightly wrapped about my knees.

They made horrendous noises as they threw me back and forth. They yelped. They howled. They growled. They bawled. They screeched and shrieked.

As I sailed across the room I saw Miss Tilly at the foot of the stairs. The horrid creatures must have seen her, too. Pitooey dropped me on the couch and fled. Phooey raced out behind him.

Miss Tilly said, "Oh, dear, honey. Were you trying to get up? You mustn't try to get up. How are you feeling?"

You ought to know, I thought.

86

I turned my head away from her and looked up at the small windows. The light was turning golden yellow. It was supper time, and no one had come to rescue me.

Hopefully Rescued

L ater, Miss Tilly came down to wash my face again. The wet rag smelled of old dish water and stale grits. When I resisted, she left. I drifted into a disquieting sleep.

After what seemed like many hours I was awakened by the sound of a muffled knock at the door upstairs. My heart leaped in hope. Someone had come. I turned my head toward the stairs and strained to listen.

Raymie!

I could scarcely make out the words, but I heard enough to know he was asking for me.

Miss Tilly's astonishing reply was, "Why, no, dear, she's not up here."

I wanted to cry out, "But I'm down here," but my throat hurt so much I couldn't get the words out.

I could tell by Raymie's voice that he was worried about me. He said, "She must be. Mama said she's here. You see, Mama sent her with a basket for you three hours ago, and she was gonna apologize to you about the trellis."

Miss Tilly's faltering voice drifted down to me.

"Well, now, let's see. My daughter, Ruthanne, is here."

There was a pause. I wondered what was happening.

"Oh, yes, you must be Miss Helene's son. Is your sister's name Marcie?"

Raymie suddenly cried out, "Why, this is my mama's basket here in the hall."

Finally I pulled from my lungs a cry for help.

"Raymie!" I called, not loudly, but loud enough for him to hear. "I'm down here."

He came barreling down those stairs. When he saw me, he gasped, "Oh, my goodness, Marcie, you look terrible. What's wrong?"

I whimpered as I held my weak, trembling arms out to him. I hadn't realized Raymie was as strong as he was. He lifted me and ran up those stairs. He had difficulty opening both the door and the gate latch, but he was aware that something was not right.

I have little memory of what happened then or on the way home. I was mostly unconscious, I think. I know Raymie rushed out the door with me, scarcely saying good-bye to Miss Tilly. I have a vague recollection of her following us out to the car, and the fat, blurred form of Jean, right behind her, huffing and puffing. They were both blurred. What could be wrong? My eyes weren't behaving correctly. And I'm not certain that the rest really happened.

I think I remember Miss Tilly was waving a bony finger and saying, "Come back to see me again, honey."

Papa's car was old, and he and Raymie often had trouble with it. In my semiconscious state, I thought that Raymie was having trouble getting the old thing started.

He turned the key in the ignition. Then he pulled the choke.

Cuh chunk, cuh chunk. The engine stopped.

I murmured, "Please, Raymie. Hurry."

Miss Tilly's horrible face was at the car window. Was that her ghostly companion hovering nearby? Everything was hazy and unreal.

The engine turned once.

Cuh chunk.

Then twice.

Cuh chunk, cuh chunk.

And finally, *cuh chunk, chunk, chunk, chunk chunk* as we headed down Sea Trout Lane.

I didn't turn to look at Miss Tilly and her haunted house. I closed my eyes and leaned back. The horrible experience was behind me, but my head continued to pound, my throat continued to ache, I continued to be hot and feverish, and the chills had become so bad now my teeth chattered.

As ill as I seemed to be I was more than relieved to have been rescued by my wonderful, fabulous, absolutely terrific brother.

Why Won't Someone Believe Me?

T he day was almost over when we arrived
home, the bayou a black mirror reflecting
the brilliant colors of the twilight sky. For some
reason I remember the beauty of that sunset now,
but at the time my thinking was fuzzy, and if I
had any thoughts they had to do with getting into
our house.

Raymie helped me up the steps and into the
house. "You ought to get Mama to take your
temperature," he said. "You look awful."

Mama took one look at me and said, "Why,
Marcie, are you all right? Miss Tilly called to say
she thinks you got sick eating too much pound
cake and too many petit fours. Do you feel like
throwing up?"

"Kinda," I said, but nausea wasn't my biggest
problem. I sat on the couch and plopped over on

the pillows. I could no longer stand. Mama rushed over to me.

She quickly placed her hand on my forehead and almost shouted, "Oh, good gracious, Marcie. You are hotter than a firecracker."

I knew what was going on as she gave me something to make the fever go down, removed my clothing, and poured lukewarm water into the bathtub.

As she helped me into the tub she let out a little scream.

Weakly, I managed to ask, "What? What's the matter?"

"Why, you have the measles. All over."

I looked down at my chest and arms. I was covered with red splotches. Why, I really was sick. I wanted to say, "I told you so," and I wished I could say that Miss Tilly had cast a spell on me, but I was too weak to talk now. I'd tell her about that in the morning. All I wanted now was my clean, comforting bed.

I lay on the pillows and let Mama pamper me. I let her put my clean, dimity nightgown over my head as if I were a tiny baby. I took the fever medicine and tried to eat the crushed ice she said would help my parched tongue. She kissed my forehead and turned on the electric fan.

That was the last thing I remembered for the next four days. During those days I slipped in and out of consciousness while Mama cared for me.

Once I heard Papa and Raymie come up from the shop, and even as ill as I was I was pleased to hear Mama say to them, "Now, y'all keep the radio down. Marcie's very ill and needs to sleep."

Sometimes I'd see Mama or Dr. Ashland bending over me, but their faces were vague and shadowy, their voices distorted. Once Mama's face faded into a likeness of Miss Tilly, and I cried out. And when Dr. Ashland moved me in the bed, Mama said I screamed, "I don't wanna play ball with you, Pitooey. Please."

When I was much better Mama told me I'd had a "really bad case of measles," and Dr. Ashland had been worried about me. I know Mama was worried; she scarcely slept during those days before the worst part of the illness was over.

Raymie and Papa came in to visit me every night before supper. Papa brought cold drinks from the shop. Once Raymie bought an iced watermelon from the ice plant. Mama let me eat some of it in my bed on a tray. Everyone was kind and considerate, so I suppose I was kind of spoiled with all that attention.

On the fifth day, I think, Mama said I could eat supper with the family in the kitchen. I was weak and unsteady, but I looked forward to getting out of my room for a while.

Before supper Raymie came to my room and sat on the bed. He pulled my ear and said, "Well, too bad. You're gonna live, shrimp."

94

I knew he was glad I was getting well, so I didn't mind his teasing remarks.

"Weren't you just scared to death of Miss Tilly and those ghosts?" I asked.

He cocked his head and looked at me with a quizzical expression. "You still talking about that ole lady being a witch? My goodness, Marcie, I can't believe you didn't see how wrong you were. She's just an ole lady. She wouldn't hurt you."

I was indignant.

"You must be outta your head," I said. "Tell me, Mr. Big Shot, if you didn't think something mighty fishy was going on, why did you come running down those stairs like crazy to get me? You were as scared as I was."

"I know," Raymie said. "That was stupid of me. But it was the way you sounded. The way you looked. You'd have thought you'd seen a ghost. I'm embarrassed at how rude I must have been to that poor ole lady."

"I did see a ghost," I cried. "I saw three ghosts, one witch, and two . . . goblins. And I'm sure of one thing. *You* must have seen that fat ghost, Jean, following us."

He lifted his eyes to heaven the way people do when they think someone really *is* out of her mind.

"There weren't any ghosts," he said. "You were delirious."

I turned away from him, angry. "I'm sorry I

thought you were so wonderful for coming to get me," I snapped.

He gave a short laugh and tried to pull my ear again.

"Don't touch me," I whined as I pulled away.

He shrugged as he left the room. "If you can't realize you were delirious, I'll have to say again, Marcie, you have one *big* imagination."

I sat up in bed, folded my arms, and pressed my lips together tightly, Mama-like.

"Nyaa, nyaa, nyaa," I said.

He just didn't want anyone to know he was afraid. Well, he'd better not tell Mama and Papa it was my imagination. I'd had enough of that.

At supper, while we were waiting for Papa to come to the table, I said, "Mama, Raymie doesn't believe that I saw ghosts and goblins at Miss Tilly's, and that she really is a witch."

Mama looked up sharply. She put a hand on my shoulder. With clear and distinct words she said, "Marcie, you have an amazing imagination that made you dream up vampires and warlocks and witches. When you became ill at Miss Tilly's your delirium sort of 'fed' on your fears, and you hallucinated because of a very high fever. Now, that's the truth, and it's final."

"It was real," I insisted. "I didn't imagine it."

I couldn't wait for Papa to wash his hands at the sink, sit down, put his napkin on his lap, and say the blessing.

The moment he said, "Amen," I started talking.

"Papa," I said in a tangled rush of words, "Mama and Raymie don't believe I really had a terrible experience with ghosts and goblins at Miss Tilly's. They don't understand why I was so scared. I thought I was gonna have to live there all my life, but Raymie came and—"

I've said that Papa was a kind and sensitive man. But I still can't believe what he did this time; he laughed. He actually *laughed*.

"Good gracious, Marcie," he said.

He was trying to stop laughing, and that made me even more furious.

"Papa!" I cried, accusingly.

He straightened his smile and put his big, work-worn hand over mine tenderly. "I'm sorry I laughed, honey," he said. "I'm sure being delirious must have been a terrible experience for you."

But when he added, "Whoo-eee, you sure do have some imagination!" I felt a hateful stone forming in my heart.

Miss Tilly
Comes to Call

The following day Jeanné came to see me. She'd had the measles when she was little, so she couldn't catch them from me.

As I've said, one reason Jeanné was my best friend was because she always believed me. She never said the events and people I told her about were "in my head." She wanted to know all about my visit to the haunted house. I told her everything.

Her eyes were bigger than ever when she said, "As soon as you get well I want to go back with you."

"Never," I said, and I meant it. "When you get older, Jeanné, you'll understand why I would never let you go through such a horrid experience."

I was six months older than Jeanné. Sometimes I let her know that. Besides, I felt I had matured a great deal lately.

"Do you know what I think?" I said.

She shook her head, spellbound.

"I think she cast a measles spell on me," I said.

"Really?" she asked, impressed.

"Think about it. Do you know one single other person in the Bayou who has the measles right now?"

She had to admit she didn't.

"Well." I nodded. "It was a hex, then."

The day after Jeanné came I was lying in my room, resting, when Mama came in. She raised the blinds a little. She'd kept them closed when I was really sick, because it's bad for the eyes to see bright lights when you have the measles. She fluffed my pillow and brushed my hair back. She placed a chair next to my bed.

"Marcie," she said, "you have a visitor."

"Who is it?"

She hesitated a moment and cast a quick look at the door.

"Miss Tilly," she said, her voice almost a whisper, "and I expect you to be nice to her."

She walked to the door. I didn't want to see Miss Tilly.

I said, "Mama, come back with her. Please. Stay in here with us."

"Everything will be all right. I promise." And she left the room.

A few minutes later Miss Tilly hobbled into the room. She was dressed in a white dress, yellowed from age. There were little buttons from her waist all the way up to her throat, even on this warm day. Her skirt hung to her ankles. Everything she wore had to be at least fifty years old; her clothes looked ancient.

Mama came behind her, carrying a rather large package, a box, wrapped in flowered brocade material. She placed the parcel on the table by my bed, smiled at me encouragingly, and left the room.

I swallowed. I wondered what evil magic could be hidden in that pretty package. There couldn't be anything good in it.

As worried as I was, I knew I should be polite.

"Wanna sit down?" I asked.

"Thank you, dear," she said as she painfully sat in the chair beside my bed.

She smiled at me, that same funny smile I remembered, and she said, "How are you feeling?"

"Okay," I said.

She talked as slowly as she moved. "I was worried about you, dear. I shouldn't have kept you so long."

"That's okay," I said.

"Nonsense!" she said. "Sometimes my mind's not so good anymore, Marcie. I didn't know what

to do. Thank heavens my neighbor, Jean Mulroney, passed by just then. I was so glad he could
take you down into the basement where it was
cool. And he was nice enough to call your mama
when he got home.

"I'm glad you came to visit, Marcie. I hope you
will come again. You are such a polite little girl.
Much more polite than an ole lady like me."

I'd never heard her say that much. I didn't
know what to say. Had Mr. Mulroney taken me
down to the basement? When had he called
Mama? I was getting ready to say "thank you" for
the compliment she had given me when she
started speaking again.

"I used to have a little girl like you. Ruthanne.
Did you know that?"

"Yes, Ma'am. Uh, you tole me . . . when I was,
uh, there."

"I probably called you Ruthanne, didn't I? You
remind me of her. Pretty dark eyes like she had. I
miss her very much."

Why was I beginning to feel guilty?

"Yes, Ma'am," I said.

"Now," she said, "why don't you open your
present?"

Her old hand, spotted and veined, pointed at
the package. I picked it up. The box was heavy,
and I didn't know what to do. I didn't want to open
this mysterious parcel, even though I always liked

opening packages. I sat up, my legs crossed, and held the box on my lap.

"Thank you," I said in a whisper. I believed I was getting that paralyzed throat again. I tugged at the ribbon. The bow knot gave way, but I sat there, not removing the paper. Miss Tilly smiled as she watched me.

I couldn't put this off any longer. I pulled the paper away and lifted the top from the cardboard box. There were several more packages inside, wrapped in tissue. I lifted the larger piece and removed the paper.

When I saw what was beneath the tissue I almost dropped it. Why, here was that fine china teapot . . . hand-painted with pink and lavender roses and pale green leaves.

I looked up at her and was surprised to see her eyes brimming with tears.

"You want me to have this?" I asked. My voice trembled.

"Ruthanne gave it to me for my birthday one year. Isn't it lovely? I know you like it. I saw your eyes when we had tea."

"It's the most beautifulest thing I have ever seen in my whole life," I said, forgetting correct English and everything else but Miss Tilly and her wonderful gift.

Then I remembered how terrible I'd been to Miss Tilly. How I'd thought she was a witch. How

I'd broken her trellis. "But I can't take this, Miss Tilly!" I cried.

"*Nonsense!*" she said emphatically. With shaking fingers, she unwrapped a teacup and placed it in my hand. "I want you to have it, dear."

"Oh, thank you, Miss Tilly," I breathed. "Thank you. Thank you. Thank you!"

Mama came into the room then, and I showed her the gift. I couldn't talk now. There was too much to think about, too much that didn't make sense. I wanted them to leave the room. I wanted to lie there and think.

Miss Tilly whispered, "I think she's tired, Miss Helene. I'd better go now."

Mama agreed that I was tired. She offered Miss Tilly some coffee and a piece of devil's food cake, and they went into the kitchen.

I set up the tea service on the table. In addition to the teapot there were four cups and saucers, four dessert plates, and a sugar bowl and a cream pitcher. Each piece was molded with delicate curves. I lay back on my pillow and stared at every piece. My heart swelled at the beauty of it.

Later I heard Mr. Mulroney at the door, asking if Miss Tilly was ready to go home. After they left Mama came to my room and sat on my bed.

"I'll share the tea set with you," I said. "You can use it when the Women's Missionary ladies come for tea."

"Thank you, darling," Mama said in a soft, sweet voice.

"Mama," I said in a small voice. "I wasn't lying about that afternoon. I don't understand, but I know something strange was going on."

Mama said, "Honey, Dr. Ashland does think you were delirious, and I'm convinced that's what you remember. Sometimes a high fever does that. But, Marcie, I do think your vivid imagination added a bit to your delirium."

Indignant, I said, "No, Mama, it was real. You see, she was different today. She didn't call me Ruthanne, and she didn't have ghosts with her. Maybe they live only at her house—"

Mama interrupted me. "There weren't any ghosts, dear."

"I know you'll never believe me, but . . ."

Mama just shook her head, unbelieving. She was annoyed.

I said, "She looked better today, but her hair is all scraggly, and she doesn't have any teeth. She's awful looking."

"Marcie, listen to me," Mama said firmly. She leaned over and took both of my shoulders in her hands. She looked right into my eyes.

"I know you don't believe you'll ever be that old, but you will. And so will Papa. And Raymie. And Jeanné. And me."

"No, you won't," I said. I didn't want to believe my mama would ever be that old. Mama gave me a look. "Well . . ." I thought for a moment. "Well . . . if you do, you'll comb your hair. And you'll have false teeth, and you won't walk all crooked."

"Maybe not," Mama said, "but *maybe* I'll have arthritis like she has, and my hands won't be strong enough to comb my hair. And *maybe* I won't have enough money to buy false teeth. And there may even be a girl named . . . Sally, maybe, and I'll mistakenly call her Marcie, because my mind will be worn out, and it won't be as clear as it is now. Maybe I'll be stooped and walk sideways like a crab. And maybe, just maybe, I'll be kind enough to take a treasured possession of mine, something my daughter, Marcie, has given me, to a little girl who has been very sick with the measles."

"Oh, Mama," I cried as I hugged her.

She hugged me back as she said, "Oh, yes, I think now might be a good time to tell you the reason Jake was yelling at Miss Tilly that day. You see, she couldn't understand his Cajun accent, and she's a little deaf. Then he stumbled on a rock as he moved closer to talk to her, and he sprained his arm. You know who told me? Jake. You know what he said? 'That Miss Tilly, she nice, nice ole lady.' "

"Yeah, I guess," I said, but there were some other things that still worried me. "How about that Edna Mae. She said Miss Tilly—"

"—She said Miss Tilly would help her, and

106

that poor, ole helpless lady does all she can for Edna Mae. You see, Ruthanne was Edna Mae's best friend. Good friends, like you and Jeanné. And when Edna Mae's baby died of dyptheria, Ruthanne and Miss Tilly were there for her. Edna Mae lost her mind with grief, and Miss Tilly and Ruthanne stayed by her, even when other people left her alone, called her crazy, and said they were afraid of her. Later, Ruthanne and her husband were in a car wreck. Both of them were killed. Edna Mae still seeks Miss Tilly out when she gets really bad."

"Oh, that's terrible," I said. My heart, and soul, and body ached through and through for all of them.

I thought about everything Mama had said for a long time that night. And I began to change my mind about many things.

With that change in my mind there was a change in my life.

Once a month my friends and I started going over to clean Miss Tilly's house.

The WMU ladies brought meals to her twice a week.

When she was feeling well, our family went by her house and took her to church with us.

And, I don't remember just how this got started, but I began to visit her. Sometimes I took her flowers and berries I had picked.

Sometimes I brought Pierre and Jeanné with

me. Miss Tilly would serve us tea, and petit fours, and pound cake. Even with arthritis, she'd play the piano for us. She played Chopin.

Sometimes she put a record on her old phonograph. The man on the record sang opera, but the record was so scratchy Jeanné and I thought he sounded like a wailing ghost.

And sometimes Miss Tilly took us up to her bedroom and showed us pictures of Ruthanne when she was a little girl. If the day was a little breezy, the torn lengths of white chiffon curtains billowed out and looked like a lady's flowing sleeves, the arms waving sort of ghostlike.

We came to love Miss Tilly the way we loved Mr. Jake.

But there's something I just can't help wondering about. I never said this to Mama, or Papa, or Raymie, but I couldn't help thinking that what happened that day wasn't only the measles or my imagination.

I absolutely cannot forget the Invisible Maid.

I can't forget Miss Evelyn.

I can't even forget "Overall" Jean. (Mr. Jean Mulroney is an awfully fat man. I've often wondered about that.)

I remember them as if I were sitting in Miss Tilly's living room only yesterday.

It's possible the high fever from the measles may have caused that game of catch. Jeanné told me when she had the measles she had a terrible headache; she thought she was a rubber ball being bounced on the sidewalk by her brother. I can see how a pounding headache would do that to a person.

So . . . maybe I was delirious.

Maybe, along with a case of measles, I did have a case of exaggerated imagination.

Maybe I'll even become a writer someday.

But I believe the rest really and truly happened.

Maybe.

Well, anyway, Jeanné believed me.

About the Author

Betty Hager never did believe in ghosts, but she *loved* being frightened. She hasn't forgotten the zinging chills she felt as a child when she was out at night in her little Alabama town. She remembers the blackness of the bayou, the eerie sounds of bullfrogs and crickets, and the sad calls of marsh hens.

Betty was eight years old when she became hooked on writing. Although she majored in writing at the University of Alabama, she didn't pursue her writing in earnest until years later. When the youngest of her three sons graduated from high school, she wrote *Old Jake and the Pirate's Treasure* and also began to write children's musicals.

Miss Tilly and the Haunted Mansion is the second book in Betty's Tales from the Bayou series. She hopes you will read all four books about Marcie and her older brother, Raymie.

Betty loves to hear from her readers. You may write her at this address:

Betty Hager
Author Relations
Zondervan Publishing House
Grand Rapids, MI 49530

Look for more of Marcie's adventures!

Old Jake and the Pirate's Treasure
Book 1 $4.99 0-310-38401-X

Is Old Jake really hiding a pirate's treasure map?
Marcie, Raymie, and Hank decide to find out —
by sneaking inside Old Jake's house! They're on
to a mystery and more ...

Miss Tilly and the Haunted Mansion
Book 2 $4.99 0-310-38411-7

Marcie imagines all sorts of things, like maybe
Miss Tilly really is a witch. When her mother
makes her visit Miss Tilly, some terrifying
adventures and a new friend await her ...

Marcie and the Shrimp Boat Adventure
Book 3 $4.99 0-310-38421-4

Marcie's brother gets to do so much — like go
sailing on the shrimp boat. So when Marcie finally
gets on board, she's overjoyed. But soon she finds
she needs a miracle to get out alive ...

Marcie and the Monster of the Bayou
Book 4 $4.99 0-310-38431-1

Marcie is sure she saw a monster, but the only
person who doesn't laugh is also telling awful
stories about Marcie's new friend. Soon Marcie
must face a bigger enemy — a hurricane.